ONCE upon a time
a few brave pilots
in little planes
flew the Air Mail.

For Bo, Peggy
and Susanna

Thanks to Jakob Stegelmann,
Stephen Walsh, Nikolaj Scherfig,
Ted Dewan, Helen Cooper
and Piet Schreuders
for all their help.

SADIE THE AIR MAIL PILOT
A DAVID FICKLING BOOK 978 0 385 60506 9
{from January 2007}
0 385 60506 4

Published in Great Britain by David Fickling Books,
a division of Random House Children's Books

This edition published 2007

1 3 5 7 9 10 8 6 4 2

DAVID FICKLING BOOKS
31 Beaumont Street, Oxford, OX1 2NP
a division of RANDOM HOUSE CHILDREN'S BOOKS
61-63 Uxbridge Rd, London W5 5SA
A division of The Random House Group Ltd.

RANDOM HOUSE AUSTRALIA [PTY] LTD
20 Alfred Street, Milsons Point, Sydney,
New South Wales 2061, Australia

RANDOM HOUSE NEW ZEALAND LTD
18 Poland Road, Glenfield, Auckland 10, New Zealand

RANDOM HOUSE [PTY] LTD
Isle of Houghton, Corner Boundary Road & Carse O'Gowrie,
Houghton 2198, South Africa

THE RANDOM HOUSE GROUP Limited Reg. No. 954009
www.kidsatrandomhouse.co.uk

A CIP catalogue record for this book is available from
the British Library.

Printed in China

www.sadiethepilot.com

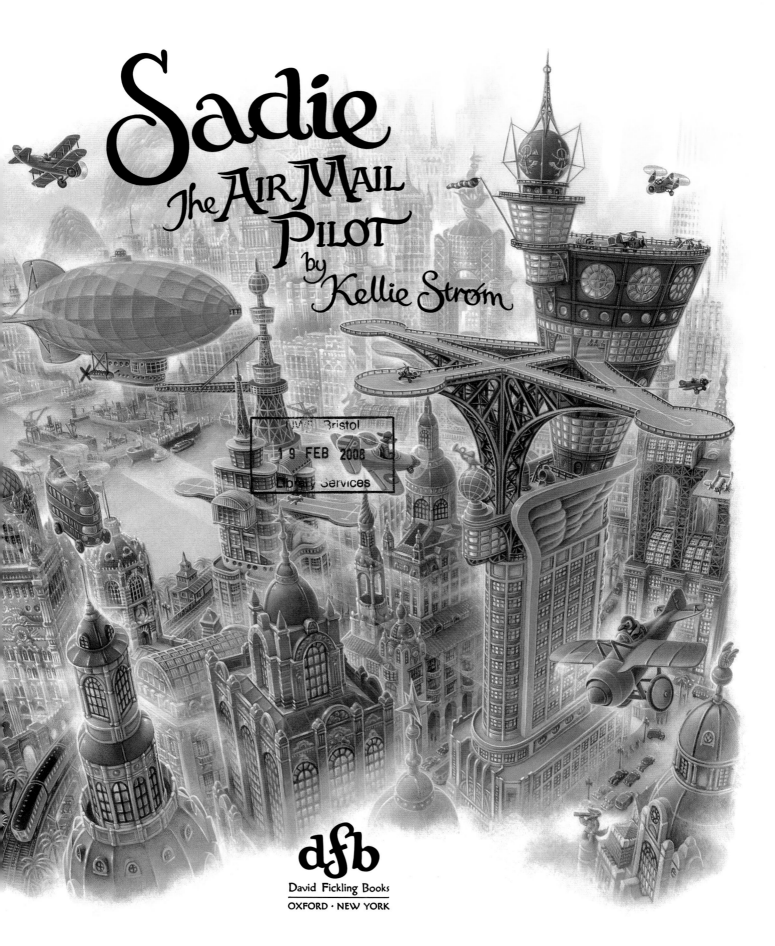

Sadie
The AIR MAIL PILOT
by Kellie Strøm

dfb

David Fickling Books

OXFORD · NEW YORK

Early one morning at Air Mail HQ, the Chief was giving orders to every pilot on the base . . . well almost every pilot.

"Pete, you fly the mail to Lima, Gus, you go to Santiago, and Charlie to Córdoba."

"Jack and Barney, you two
do the route to Panama,
and Sadie . . . "
But Sadie wasn't there.
"WHERE'S SADIE?!"

"PILOT SADIE! WAKE UP!"

"Yikes!" cried Sadie as she fell from her hammock.

"You're late again," growled the Chief.

"Remember the oath of the Air Mail Service:

No wind, no rain, no cold or flu,
Can stop the Air Mail getting through!"

"Now, you've got a mission to fly," he told her,
"all the way to Knuckle Peak Weather Station."
   "Yes sir! Right sir! I'm ready!" said Sadie.
   "I'll get your breakfast," said Mickey the mechanic.
   "No time to eat!" said the Chief. "Get dressed and go!"

Sadie checked her route-map.
"Oh my!" said Mickey,
"those mountains look tricky."
"Don't you worry," said
Sadie, "I could fly there
with my eyes shut!"

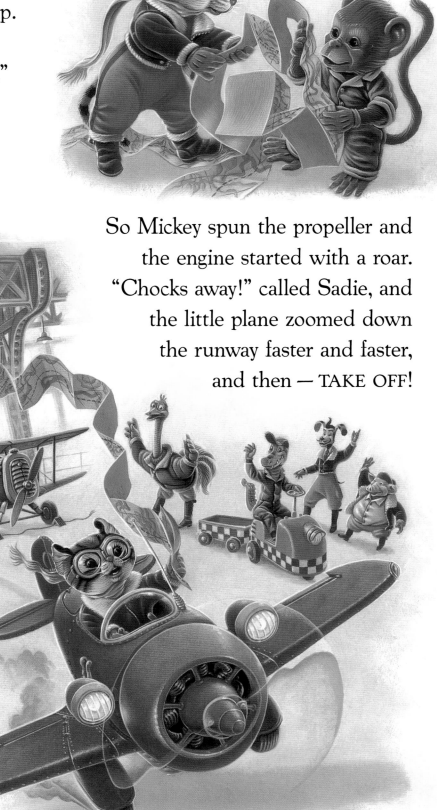

So Mickey spun the propeller and
the engine started with a roar.
"Chocks away!" called Sadie, and
the little plane zoomed down
the runway faster and faster,
and then — TAKE OFF!

Out past the city she flew, over coffee farms and banana trees, over forests and rivers and hills . . .

. . . out and beyond and up and
away to the far away mountains.

But as the mountains came into view, dark clouds filled the sky.

Sadie radioed ahead to the Weather Station.

"Calling Knuckle Peak, come in Knuckle Peak! What's the forecast — over?"

Way up on Knuckle Peak
a wild wind was blowing.
  Weatherbird Gusty
called Sadie back: "This is
Knuckle Peak — Knuckle Peak
to Pilot! A storm is coming —
return to base! Repeat, return
to base!"
  "Rotten luck!" said
Forecaster Fogg. "Nobody
could fly here in weather
like this."

But Sadie wasn't ready to give up.
"Turn back? Well swipe my stripes — no!
Sadie the Pilot is on the job, and the
Air Mail is going to get through!

Things look grim, but don't get nervous,
Nothing scares the Air Mail Service!"

Then up she flew, straight up
and into the dark clouds.

Suddenly she heard a loud growl.
Was it thunder? Was it the engine?
No, that was Sadie's empty stomach!
 "I hope they've got lunch ready
when I get there," she thought.

GRROWL!

rudder

port navigation light

elevator

tail light

flap

aileron

fuel tank

radial engine

starboard navigation light

Sadie's plane twisted and turned through the clouds, just missing the rocky cliffs on every side.

At last she saw Knuckle Peak, and the Weather Station way up on top.

"She made it!" called Fogg.

"Such a brave pilot!" said Gusty.

"Yes, or crazy maybe."

Sadie unloaded the mail. There were lots of important letters for
Gusty, and magazines, parcels and a mail-order catalogue.

There was an envelope for Fogg too.

"It's a letter from my sweetheart — ah Julieta!"

And while Sadie ate a bowl of warm soup, Fogg wrote a reply.

Then the wind outside gave a howl!
"The storm is getting worse!" warned Gusty.
"Don't fly now, Sadie. Stay here 'til it blows over."
But Sadie took Fogg's letter to Julieta and
swore the oath of the Air Mail Service:

*"The winds may blow ice and snow,
But still the Air Mail's got to go!"*

Down into the raging storm she flew,
and the wind whistled in her ears
and the cold rattled her teeth.

Sadie's whiskers were frozen blue — the plane's wings were freezing up too! She tried to scrape off the ice, but the wind blew all the worse.

"SOS, Mayday!" she called into her radio. "I'm going down!"

With all her strength she tried to steer the plane — but NO! The controls were frozen solid — "HELP! HELP!" cried Sadie. "I'm going to . . ."

CRASH!

Sadie opened her eyes and looked around. Her plane was stuck in the snow. Her radio was broken. "What will happen?" she thought, "I could be lost forever — I could starve!"

"HELP!" she called, "HELP!"
But only her echo answered,
"HELP . . . HELP . . . HELP . . ."
And the wind howled
like a terrible wild creature,
a wailing mountain monster,
coming closer, and closer . . .

"YeeeEEK!" screamed Sadie.

But the creature spoke: "Are you OK, pilot?
I am Igor from the mountain patrol, and I have
come to rescue you!"

"Oh, my beating heart," said Sadie. "I thought
you were going to eat me!"

"Well, I *am* hungry," he said, "but luckily
I have my emergency rations." And he gave
Sadie a big bar of chocolate from his backpack.

Igor had a whole load of rescue equipment with him.

"Now, how can I help you get home?" he wondered.

"I have an idea!" said Sadie, looking at Igor's skis.

First Igor and Sadie dug her plane out of the snowdrift.

Then they tied the skis tight onto the wheels.

And at last Sadie climbed
aboard and tried
the engine.

"Vra-HOOM!"
roared the engine! Sadie steered
down the slope and flew into the air.
   "THANK YOU FOR THE SKIS!" she yelled
down to Igor. "I'LL MAIL YOU SOME NEW ONES!"
   Then she turned her plane towards home . . .

. . . and flew back across the mountains,
back over forests, and rivers, and hills . . .

. . . over banana trees, and coffee farms,
all the way to the city, and Air Mail HQ.

"YAY!"

All the pilots cheered as Sadie came sliding down the runway.

"I've got your supper ready!" called Mickey.

Yes, at the end of a hard day, all a pilot wants is a good meal and a good sleep . . .

. . . but wait, here's the Chief with more parcels to send, and uh-oh, he's got Sadie down for the job!

Over mountains high and oceans deep,
The Air Mail Service never sleeps!